MW01114168

Chepecho and Her Clippity, Flappity, Floppity Friends

Written by Meg Marino, M.D.
Illustrated by Lina Naddaf

Text copyright © 2018 by Meg Marino
Pictures copyright © 2018 by Mayaseen Publishing LLC

Michigan, U.S.A.

All rights reserved. No part of the book may be reproduced in any form
without prior written permission except in the case of brief quotations
embodied in articles for review.

www.mayaseen.com

First Edition
Library of Congress Control Number: 2018950987
ISBN 978-1-946131-23-2

Printed in Oman

Chepecho
and Her
Clippity
Flappity
Floppity
Friends

Meg Marino, M.D.

Illustrated by Lina Naddaf

مياسين
Mayaseen

Chepecho lives on an island.
She has two legs for running,
two wings for flying,
and a tail for swimming.
She loves running,
flying, and swimming,

but she wishes she had someone to play with.

Every morning, Chepecho watches the horses run onto the beach. The horses chase each other on the sand.

Thump-Thump, Thump-Thump.

Chepecho's hooves make that same sound. She doesn't play with the horses, because she cannot run as quickly.

The horses run back to the hills as the birds fly down to the beach. The birds chase each other in the air.

Woosh-Woosh, Woosh-Woosh.

Chepecho's wings make that same sound. She doesn't play with the birds, because she cannot fly as high.

The birds retreat to the cliffs as the sea lions swim onto the shore.
The sea lions chase each other in the water.

10

Swish-Swish, Swish-Swish.

Chepecho's tail makes that same sound. She doesn't play with the sea lions, because she cannot swim as far.

11

12

One morning, a horse runs up to Chepecho and neighs,

"Tag, you're it! Are you playing with us?"

"I don't know how," says Chepecho.

"It's easy," says the horse.
"You chase us until you tag someone.

Then you say, 'Tag, you're it!' Those are the rules."

Chepecho chases the horses. She splashes them with her wings as they play in the water. Chepecho's legs can't run as quickly as the horses' legs, but it doesn't matter. She flies to catch up to them.

"Tag, you're it!" Chepecho says.

15

Whoosh-Whoosh, Whoosh-Whoosh.

"Oh no! Here come the birds!"
neighs a horse. "Those birds are the worst!"

"Why don't you like the birds?"
asks Chepecho.

"They flap their wings everywhere,"
says the horse.

"Flippity-flappity-flap-flap-flap
all the time. What if they flap their
wings at us?"

"Are you afraid of their wings?" asks Chepecho. "My wings go whoosh-whoosh, whoosh-whoosh like a bird's wings."

"You're like a horse because you have hooves like ours. You aren't like those flappity birds," a horse explains.

"Are you coming with us?"

17

The horses run away, and the birds land on the beach. The birds chase each other in the air and splash in the water.

A bird touches Chepecho on her tail and squawks, "Tag, you're it!"

Chepecho chases the birds and splashes them with her tail. She cannot fly as high as the birds can fly, but it doesn't matter. She swims to catch up to them.

Swish-Swish, Swish-Swish.

"Oh no! Here come the sea lions!"
squawks a bird. "Those sea lions are the worst!"

"Why don't you like the sea lions?"
asks Chepecho.

"They flop their tails everywhere,"
squawks another.

"Floopity-floppity-flop-flop-flop all the
time. What if they flop their tails at us?"

"Are you afraid of their tails?" asks Chepecho. "My tail goes swish-swish, swish-swish like a sea lion's tail."

"You're like a bird because you have wings like ours. You aren't like those floppity sea lions," a bird explains.

"Are you coming with us?"

23

The birds fly away to the cliffs, and the sea lions swim to shore.

A sea lion touches Chepecho's hoof and barks,

"Tag, you're it!"

She cannot swim as far as the sea lions can swim, but it doesn't matter. She runs to catch up to them.

Thump-Thump, Thump-Thump.

"Oh no! Here come the horses!"
barks a sea lion. "Those horses are the worst."

"Why don't you like the horses?" asks Chepecho

"Those horses clop their hooves everywhere,"
barks another.
"Clippity-cloppity-clop-clop-clop all the
time. What if they clop their hooves at us?"

"Are you afraid of the horses' hooves?"asks Chepecho. "My hooves go thump-thump, thump-thump like a horse's hooves."

"You're like a sea lion because you have a tail like ours. You aren't like those cloppity horses," a sea lion explains.

"Are you coming with us?"

Woosh-Woosh, Woosh-Woosh.

The birds land on the beach.

"Go back out to sea where you belong and get your floppity tails off our beach," a bird squawks at the sea lions.

"Go back to the hills where you came from!" a sea lion barks at the horses.

"We don't want your cloppity kind here."

"Get out of here!" a horse neighs at the birds.

"Don't fly in here with your flappity wings as if you own the place. We were here first."

"Can't we all play together?"
asks Chepecho.

32

"No!" squawks a bird.
"We can't play with those floopity-floppity tails!"

"No!" barks a sea lion. "We can't play with those
clippity-cloppity hooves."

"Nay!" neighs a horse.
"We can't play with those
flippity-flappity wings."

After spending the day playing tag, Chepecho knows she belongs with the horses, the birds, and the sea lions. She doesn't see hooves and wings and tails. She sees her friends who love playing tag on the beach. Why can't they see how similar they are?

"You laughed when I used my tail to splash you in the water. Are you afraid of my tail?
You had fun chasing me in the sand when I used my hooves to run away. Are you afraid of my hooves?
You liked it when I used my wings to fly over you in the water. Are you afraid of my wings?"

Chepecho touches one of the birds.
"Tag, you're it!"

No one moves.

"I said, 'Tag, you're it!'"
Chepecho insists.

"Now you have to chase everyone.
That's the rule!"

As the sun sets, Chepecho's friends run, fly, and swim together as they play. The sounds come together like a song.

Swish-Thump-Thump-Whoosh-Whoosh,
Swish-Thump-Thump-Whoosh-Whoosh,
Swish-Thump-Thump-Whoosh-Whoosh.

As Chepecho sings along,
a horse touches Chepecho's wing.
"Chepecho, **tag, you're it!**"